THE LAND OF INBETWEEN
The Hungry Horse
Pauline Devine
Illustrations Terry Myler

THE CHILDREN'S PRESS

First published 2001 by
The Children's Press
an imprint of Anvil Books
45 Palmerston Road, Dublin 6

2 4 6 8 7 5 3 1

ISBN 1 901737 33 0

Typeset by Computertype Limited
Printed by Colour Books Limited

Contents

1 The Land of In-Between

The Land of In-Between lies beyond the earth and close to the sky.

In the west, the grass grows rich and green. It is the best grass in the world.

The east has dense forests. Evergreens, oaks, beech trees, silver birch. Every tree in the world grows there.

Once it was a peaceful and happy land, ruled by a wise old king.

The king had two sons named Huff and Puff, but when he died, Huff would not agree to rule jointly with Puff.

So they divided the land. Huff chose the east and Puff the west.

The Border was marked by a great wall. Soldiers kept watch day and night and no one dared cross it without a pass.

King Huff was tall and thin, always scowling, always in a huff. He was as dark and gloomy as his forests.

King Puff was short and fat and sunny-tempered, always out of breath, always puffing. His great pride and joy was his fleet-footed horse, Doolin.

The only part of the land that was not divided was Bald Mountain in the north. Here lived Bidden, the animal witch. So powerful were her spells that everyone was afraid of her.

When she wanted to know what was going on, she stirred the dark waters of a pool on top of the mountain. Then she could see everything.

One day she saw a great crowd gather in the grounds of Puff's palace.

'Ah,' she said. 'The annual Palace Races. Doolin against all comers!'

She flew down with her pet magpie.

2 The Race

In the palace grounds, King Puff was standing beside Doolin. The horse looked magnificent, with his shining chestnut coat and flowing cream mane.

'Nobody – or nothing – can beat Doolin,' boasted King Puff.

'Why bother having a race, then?' asked a voice from the crowd.

'Good point! It's a race to see who comes second and third. Hee! Hee!'

The witch stepped up.

'My magpie here will outrace Doolin.'

'You're mad!' laughed Puff. Then he thought, 'Why not? Let's have fun.'

He did not realise then that the woman was Bidden, the witch.

Some of the crowd laughed with him.

'What a crazy coot!' they jeered. 'A magpie against the great Doolin!'

But the old people, who recognised Bidden, crossed themselves.

She took a ball of thread from her

pocket and tied one end to Doolin's tail.
Everyone wondered what she was doing.

The race began.

Doolin was off like the wind but when
the witch pulled on the magic thread he
was forced to slow down. And, strain as
he might, he could only limp along.

The magpie won the race.

King Puff was furious. 'You cheated,'
he said to Bidden. 'How dare you cheat!'

He aimed a kick at the magpie and
knocked it to the ground.

The witch picked up the magpie, who
was only stunned, and stroked it.

Turning to Doolin, she whispered,
'Stay as you are!' Then she chanted some
strange words.

Turning to the king, she hissed, 'Now
he's no longer Doolin the Speedy. He's
Doolin the Greedy.'

She rolled her magic thread into a ball
and flew away with her magpie.

Doolin trembled and wobbled.

King Puff also trembled as he stroked
his champion horse. Too late he had
recognised Bidden.

'My poor horse,' he sobbed. 'What
awful mischief is she up to? What did
she mean by "Doolin the Greedy"?'

3 Peaky

In a corner of King Puff's kingdom, in a
small stone house, lived a boy called
Peaky. His best friends were the rabbits
who grazed his field.

One evening a rabbit poked his head
out of the grass.

'Peaky,' he said, 'you'll have to do
something. The grass is growing faster
than we can eat it.'

Peaky agreed. The recent rain had
made it grow very fast. It was now
higher than his head. It hid the windows
of his house and made it dark inside.

'You must go to the fair,' went on the rabbit, 'and get a sheep or a goat or a horse to help us keep the grass down.'

Peaky counted his valuable seashells into a bag. He had enough to buy an animal.

'We'll bring you there,' said the rabbit.

Next morning he went to the fair in a giant mushroom drawn by twelve of his friends, the rabbits. But when they got there, the fair had been cancelled. By Order of the King.

No one could say why.

In the palace, King Puff and all his ministers sat in the great hall.

From the day Bidden had cast her spell on Doolin, the horse had not only lost his gift of speed.

Now he had a huge appetite.

'What are we to do?' Puff asked his Chief Minister, looking out sadly at Doolin who was gobbling grass as hard as he could, leaving behind him heaps of smelly horse dung.

'Put him down,' said the Chief Minister. 'If you don't, he'll eat all the grass in the kingdom. Then he'll eat the crops. Then the vegetables. There will be famine. The people will starve.'

'I won't have him killed,' said the king.

'It's either your people – or Doolin,' said the Second Minister.

'Why not bring him to the Border?' said his assistant. 'We could slip him over when the soldiers aren't looking. Then he can eat Huff's grass.'

'Good thinking,' said the Chief Minister. 'Meanwhile we must avoid rumour. We don't want the people wondering where Doolin is. No crowds. Cancel all fairs.'

With a heavy heart, the king agreed.
He turned away as Doolin was led off.

But Doolin didn't stay long in King
Huff's kingdom. He didn't like the
gloomy forests (which he couldn't eat
anyway) and the grass was nothing like
as lush and plentiful as in Puff's land.

So after a day or two, he limped back
across the Border, being careful to avoid
the guards. He knew he no longer had
the speed to escape if they chased him.

4 Doolin Makes a Friend

Peaky was cutting his meadow with a
scythe when he heard the sound of a
horse's hooves. A chestnut horse, with a
flowing cream-coloured mane, brushed
past him and began to gobble the grass.

One thing puzzled Peaky about him.
For such a fine-looking horse, he moved
in a stiff and shaky way.

'Like a very old ass,' thought Peaky.

Still he was a great grass eater, so

Peaky hoped he would stay. He cleaned and brushed his coat until it shone and polished his hooves.

Soon the grass was eaten down below the window-sill of the house.

'Never seen anything like it in all my born days,' said an old rabbit. 'He crops the grass like a sheep.'

Soon it was down to its roots and the rabbits had to go next door for supper.

But Doolin went on eating.

When the grass was finished, he ate the hedges and bushes. Then he eyed the field beside them.

'Open the gate, Peaky,' he said. 'I'm still hungry. I want more grass.'

'Who are you?' asked Peaky. 'Why have you such a huge appetite?'

'My name is Doolin. I'm King Puff's champion racehorse. Once I was faster than the wind. But, alas, a spell was put on me and I can no longer run. All I know is that I must keep on eating.'

18

As he spoke, he was devouring the thistles and docks along the wayside.

'Who put the spell on you?'

'Bidden,' said Doolin.

He told Peaky about the race and how the witch had put him under a spell.

'We must find Bidden and make her remove the spell,' said Peaky.

'No chance of that!' Doolin's voice was gloomy.

'We'll have to try. Where does she live?'

'On top of Bald Mountain.'

'Then we must find the way there.'

5 The Three Good Deeds

Soon after they set out, they came to a farmhouse. The woman there did not know the way to Bald Mountain.

Peaky asked for some milk but she said, 'We would gladly give it to you if we had any. But our cow is dry.' Her voice grew low. 'It's the witch!'

Peaky saw that the bell around the cow's neck was cracked. 'Get her a new one and the milk will flow again.'

Further on, they saw a frog floating on a leaf in a pond.

'Help me!' he cried. 'I've forgotten how to swim! It's the witch!'

Peaky threw his cap into the pond. The frog jumped into it and sailed safely to dry land.

'When you go into the water again,' said Peaky, 'you'll be able to swim.'

The frog was very grateful but he did not know the way to Bald Mountain.

Then Peaky saw a swallow overhead.

'Help me!' it twittered. 'I've lost my way. I must go south. If I don't get there before the winter, I'll die.'

'Fly into the wind,' said Peaky, 'and you'll reach the south.'

Then he shouted, 'First, tell us the way to Bald Mountain.'

'Turn left at the cross-roads before you reach the border town of Pluto. That will bring you there.'

'Three good turns today,' said Peaky. 'Surely our luck will turn. And now we know how to get to Bald Mountain.'

6 The Spell

High on Bald Mountain the witch was uneasy. Her big toe was burning.

That meant something was wrong.

She hopped over to the pool and looked into the waters. She could see towns, villages, fields and people.

Suddenly she saw Doolin and a small boy with a peaked cap walking the pathways near the Border. She heard everything that was said and she grew angry.

23

'So they want to call on me. Get me to lift the curse on Doolin. The cheek of them! Don't they know no one ever gets to Bald Mountain! Ever!'

She thought for a while, then hissed, 'I'll change Doolin's colour so that Peaky won't recognise him. If they're separated, that will be the end of that!'

Peaky and Doolin soon came to the cross-roads near Pluto and took the left road. Then a strange thing happened. No matter how many times they tried, they always found themselves back at the cross-roads.

Finally Peaky decided they should go into Pluto and inquire there.

Near the town they read a notice that had just been put up.

'It's not safe for you to be seen,' said Peaky to Doolin. 'I'll try and find out what is happening. You stay here until I come back.'

There was a small inn just outside the town. Peaky crept up and listened to the talk within.

'Poor Doolin,' one voice was saying, 'He won't escape this time.'

'Indeed no,' said another. 'As soon as it was known that he had left King Huff's kingdom, King Puff's ministers ordered that he must be found.'

'What will they do to him?'

'Kill him, of course. They say that if he is left alive there will be no grass in the kingdom. There will be famine.'

'I heard tell once that the cure for any curse that the witch Bidden casts is to be found on Bald Mountain.'

'But nobody can get to Bald
Mountain. Everyone knows that.'

'Except those who were born there.
The red fox was born on Bald Mountain.
He could take you there.'

'It would be a brave man who would
dare to call on Bidden!'

Peaky slipped away. The cure for
Doolin's malady was to be found on Bald
Mountain. But he now knew he could not
find his own way there. He would have
to find the red fox.

7 A Change of Colour

When Peaky had gone, Doolin, still hungry, went into a meadow to graze. There he met a white farm horse. His owner had turned him loose from the wagon to rest before they crossed the Border.

As the two horses grazed, a thick, dark cloud hovered over them. The witch was making her spell. The horses nodded off to sleep and the cloud dropped down and hid them from view.

When Doolin awoke he found his coat had turned white. The white horse had also changed colour – he was chestnut!

When the farmer came back, he harnessed up the white horse (not knowing it was Doolin) and shooed away the other horse.

When the witch looked into her pool and saw Doolin being driven away, she was delighted. 'That's the end of him! He'll spend his days eating the farmer out of house and home until they get rid of him. Peaky will never find him now.'

Then she gave a great yawn. 'It's time I took a bit of a holiday. I'm overworked, I really am.' So then and there she packed her red apron and very soon she was airborne, the magpie in her pocket, heading for the Rim of the World to visit her cousin and freshen up her spells.

Soon after the farmer drove away with Doolin, a crowd of people spotted a chestnut horse grazing in a meadow. Not knowing that it was the farmer's white horse, they thought it was Doolin. He was led away to the slaughter house.

Only that his colour changed back to white by morning, he would have been dead meat. As the people were scratching their heads, wondering what was afoot, he broke free and galloped away towards the Border.

Shortly after he caught up with the farmer and Doolin, who had changed back to his old chestnut colour. The farmer was looking amazed!

'Thank God you're back,' he said to the white horse. 'I knew this other fellow wasn't you. He has about as much strength as a kitten. And he never stops eating!'

He unharnessed Doolin and let him go. Then he and the white horse trotted off.

Doolin knew he was lucky to be alive. The witch had unwittingly saved his life.

When Peaky came back from the inn he couldn't find Doolin. So he began to search for him. He met the rabbits of the mushroom and told them his story.

'We'll take you to the red fox of Bald Mountain,' they said. 'He'll be able to find Doolin. He knows everything that goes on in the Land of In-Between.'

They carried him to the foot of Bald Mountain. There they met the red fox. He told them about the witch's spell, about the horses changing colour and how Doolin had escaped with his life.

'I've seen him this morning,' said the red fox. 'He was wandering around near the Border. Then King Huff's daughter took him away to the castle.'

'We'll go and find him,' said Peaky.

As they were leaving, Peaky admired the grass that grew up around them. 'The grass on Bald Mountain,' the red fox told him, 'is richer and better than that anywhere else in either kingdom.'

'I'll take a bunch with me,' said Peaky. 'Doolin is sure to be hungry.'

8 Princess Pom Pom

Princess Pom Pom, King Huff's only
child, saw Doolin grazing at the wayside
where the farmer had left him. She
ordered her carriage to stop and out she
skipped.

Now the princess was very beautiful,
with long golden hair and big blue eyes.
She was also very clever. Her teachers
had taught her very little – which was as

much as they knew – but she made up
for this by reading every book in the
castle library. Very often twice!

'Beautiful!' she said when she saw
Doolin. 'He has the head of an Arab
horse. Take him to the Royal Stables.'

'But, Princess,' said the servants, 'this
is only an old working horse...'

'Do as I say!' said the princess, who
had very royal manners.

So they tied Doolin to the carriage
with a long lead and took him along.

'*Another* horse!' grumbled King Huff when the princess told him about Doolin.

'Not one like this,' said the princess.

So King Huff was dragged down to the Royal Stables.

Something about the horse struck him. He asked the Stablemaster, who said, 'Why, that's Doolin, King Puff's famous champion horse. I saw him at...'

He had been about to say 'at race meetings'. Then he remembered that the subjects of King Huff were not allowed to visit Puff's kingdom. So he coughed and hoped he wouldn't be asked where.

But Huff was only interested in
Doolin. He now had Puff's great horse.
His eyes gleamed.

'We'll have a super race-meeting,' he
said. 'Doolin, now my horse, will race
against all comers.'

'But, your Majesty,' began the Royal
Stablemaster, 'this horse is no good.'

'What do you mean?' said Huff in a
fury. 'Do you think I don't know about
Doolin, the horse who has never been
beaten?'

The truth was that Huff spent all his
time sitting in his great castle brooding
about his enemies. He never read a book

or a paper, never turned on the radio or
switched on TV. He already knew everything, or so he thought. He felt anything
he didn't know wasn't worth knowing.

So, although all his courtiers and
servants and his people, rich and poor,
knew the sad story of Doolin, he didn't.

So the order went out and no one dared
to question it. There was to be a great
race-meeting. Doolin against all comers.

Poor Doolin trembled when he heard
the news. 'What will become of me when
I fail?' he thought.

He didn't say 'if'. He said 'when'.

When King Puff heard about the race-meeting, tears flowed down his cheeks.

'Oh, my poor Doolin,' he wept. 'That idiot Huff doesn't know he's lost his speed. He'll lose the race and Huff will be so enraged at losing face that he'll have him put down. I must save him. I'll go and see King Huff!'

The Royal Ministers were aghast.

'You can't,' they all cried together. 'Kings don't call on each other. It's against Court Protocol.'

'That's enough,' shouted Puff. 'You talked me into getting rid of Doolin. I'm not going to listen to you any more. Bring me my carriage.'

9 The Magic Grass

Meanwhile Peaky had arrived at King Huff's castle in the East Kingdom. He had with him the grass he had gathered on Bald Mountain.

But when he arrived before the golden gates, he was stopped by the guards.

'Be off, young fellow,' jeered one. 'This is a castle. Not for urchins like you.'

'No admittance except on business,' sniggered another.

Peaky took off his cap and said in a humble voice, 'Brave, strong men who keep people out but let people in, could I have the job of looking after the horses?'

That made them laugh even more.

'You are much too small for such work,' sneered the head guard. 'A horse might stand on you. Off with you!'

'Just a moment,' came a clear young voice from inside the gates.

It was Princess Pom Pom who was bringing some hot soup to the gate-keeper's wife who was ill.

She looked at Peaky.

'Are you fond of animals?'

'Yes. Very.'

'Then you can have the job.'

The guards scowled but they had to let him in and direct him to the stables.

'Oh, Doolin!' cried Peaky when he saw the great horse. 'I've found you!'

'Just in time,' said Doolin gloomily. 'This King Huff thinks I'm Doolin the Speedy. When he finds out I'm not, he'll kill me.'

'He won't. I'll tell him your story.'

'You can't. Nobody here dare talk of anything to do with King Puff.'

As he was talking, he was sniffing at Peaky's bundle of grass, the grass from Bald Mountain.

He took a mouthful or two. His ears began to quiver. Waves of strength were passing through his body. Peaky sprang back as the horse's front hooves began to paw restlessly at the ground.

At last Doolin bounded from the earth and came crashing down on all fours with a thud that shook the stable yard. Neck and tail arched, he burst into a gallop.

Through the stable door he raced and round and round the paddock outside.

'It's the grass!' cried Peaky. 'It has given him back his speed!'

All the animals in the kingdom stopped to listen to those drumming hooves. But even as they listened, the sound died away.

Doolin returned to his stable at his old slow limp.

'We must get more grass,' said Peaky to the red fox, who had followed him to the stables. 'We'll set out at once.'

10 King Puff Arrives

When King Puff's carriage drew up
before the gates of King Huff's castle,
his Chief Minister beside him, the guards
didn't know what to do.

'Have you got a pass?' one asked.

'A pass!' shouted Puff. 'Kings don't
have passes. King Huff is my brother,
and even though we haven't seen each
other for years, I know he'll greet me
with open arms. And send you lot to the
deepest dungeon.'

'If they don't let him in,' thought the terrified minister, 'he'll lose his temper and go to war and we'll all be killed. Why didn't I stay at home?'

But the guards were having second thoughts. It was a *very* splendid carriage.

'Maybe we should let him in. After all he's a king.'

'And he says he's Huff's brother.'

So they opened the gates.

'First to the stables,' ordered Puff.

There they found Doolin and Peaky.

'My poor Doolin,' said the king. 'Where have you been? Oh, how I've missed you.' He fell on the horse's neck and began to weep.

'He has been wandering around, homeless, ever since he left you,' said Peaky.

'Oh, those stupid ministers,' said the king. 'They're not worth a row of beans. I'll sack them when I get back.'

He looked at the horse, who seemed to be every inch the Doolin of old.

Then he became sad again.

'But what's this about racing? He can't race. He's lost his speed.'

'It comes back when we feed him the grass from Bald Mountain,' explained Peaky. 'And we have enough here to last for the race.'

'Brill!' said King Puff. 'My lad, you have more brains in your little finger than all those silly advisers I have. I'm appointing you my top minister from this day forth.'

'You can't,' cried the Chief Minister. 'He's only a stable boy. He couldn't handle Affairs of State.'

'Get stuffed,' said the king. 'Anyone who can manage Doolin can manage a kingdom.'

11 The Bet

A large grandstand had been erected on the wide plain beside the castle. Strings of coloured bunting hung everywhere and over all was the flag of the East Kingdom.

A huge crowd of people had assembled for the races, and as Peaky and Doolin approached they fell back in wonder. None of them had ever seen such a magnificent horse before.

The band struck up a fanfare as King Huff and Princess Pom Pom arrived at the Royal Box.

At that moment, King Puff dashed up and threw his arms around his brother.

'Thank God for this day,' he said. 'After all those years, we're going to be friends again.' He held out a hand.

'Not so fast,' scowled King Huff. 'Who says we'll be friends again. I don't want you as a friend.'

'Father,' said the princess, stepping
between them, 'take the hand he offers.
If you don't, I'll go and stay with him.'

At this, King Huff, who dearly loved
his daughter though he never showed it,
was visibly upset.

'Tell you what,' said King Puff. 'We'll
have a bet. If I win, we'll be friends. If
you win, we'll stay enemies.'

'What kind of a wager?' asked Huff.

'Why not a race?' said the princess.
'King Puff's horse Doolin against any
horse in our stables.'

52

'But Doolin is now my...' began Huff.
Then he stopped.

Last night he had overheard two of his
servants talking about Doolin and the
curse of Bidden. So he had secretly
gone to the stables.

What he saw was a tired old horse,
barely able to move.

He thought of calling off the races but
the people were already gathering. Then
he decided he would announce that Doolin
was ill. But Doolin clearly was not ill.

So he was in a state of panic when Huff appeared. Now he saw a way out.

'You're on,' he said. 'Let me send to the stables for a horse to race Doolin.'

Princess Pom Pom, who knew her father well, suspected a trick. Only last night he had been boasting that Doolin was now his and that he would race him.

She took Peaky aside and they talked for a few minutes. When she came back, she was beaming.

Peaky led Doolin to the start, all the time feeding him more of the mountain grass. The princess clapped her hands.

'Let the race begin!'

There was a hush as the two horses
set off. The silence grew as Doolin tore
around the course, a blur against the
rails.

He finished way out in front.

King Huff scowled and cried aloud,
'Trickery! That horse wasn't able to run
last night.'

'So that's why you let King Puff have
him!' said the princess sweetly. 'You
thought he had lost his speed. You are
well served for your treachery.'

'Let's not quarrel again,' said Puff.
'All's fair in love and war. Doolin won.
Now I ask you to be friends.'

Again he held out his hand.

At first Huff hesitated. Then his eye
fell on Princess Pom Pom. Slowly he
took the outstretched hand.

'Hurray,' shouted the crowd and the
sky grew dark as hundreds of caps were
thrown into the air.

But Peaky led Doolin away. The effect
of the grass had worn off and Doolin was
once again his tired old self.

12 The Ever After

Bidden was flying low over King Huff's kingdom on her way home.

'What's going on here?' she thought.

She dropped down behind a rock on the edge of the racecourse.

Doolin, who was passing by, suddenly reared up. Peaky spied Bidden and, with the aid of some guards, dragged her, screaming and kicking, before the kings.

Both agreed she must be locked up.

But Princess Pom Pom spoke up.

'She's not really bad,' she said. 'She

has a great gift for healing. Only instead of using it for good, she has used it to make mischief. I will be her friend and help her.'

'Me, too,' said Peaky. 'But first she must give Doolin back his speed.'

Bidden wiped away a tear:

I took Doolin's gift of speed
  I am ashamed to say.
I wound it in a ball of thread
  And tossed it far away.
It was a wicked, clever deed
  And I wish I could undo it.
But I cannot now recall
  Exactly where I threw it.

Suddenly there was a loud flutter from Bidden's apron pocket. A shiny beak appeared, followed by two black eyes.

It was the magpie – who never threw anything away. He flew back to his nest and got the ball of thread.

Bidden tied one end to Doolin's tail and chanted:

Thread, thread, do your good deed,
Give Doolin back his Gift of Speed.

In the castle King Puff and King Huff were having supper.

'I started the quarrel,' said Huff. 'Take my crown. I'm not fit to wear it.'

'No,' said Puff. 'I was a bad king. I enjoyed myself and left everything to my ministers. You take my crown.'

'Why not rule together?' suggested the princess. 'Then you can keep an eye on one another.'

The two kings agreed. Then Huff turned to Peaky. 'Young man, my people and I owe you much. Not to mention Doolin. As I have no family, you will be my heir.'

'Your Majesty,' said Peaky, 'this is all in the future. Now I must go back to my meadow. The grass will have grown high again.'

'Well, Doolin won't be able to eat it all now,' chuckled King Puff. 'I'll send over a flock of sheep!'

*

In the fullness of time, Peaky married Princess Pom Pom and they became heirs to the Land of In-Between.

Bidden became famous for healing sick animals.

As for Doolin, the fleet-footed, he never tired of racing like the wind. Nor has any animal galloped faster anywhere since or before.

A Little about **Elephants**

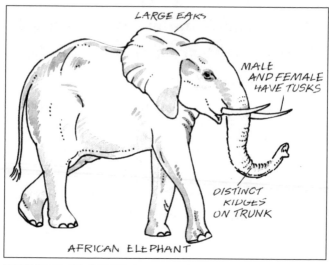

LARGE EARS

MALE AND FEMALE HAVE TUSKS

DISTINCT RIDGES ON TRUNK

AFRICAN ELEPHANT

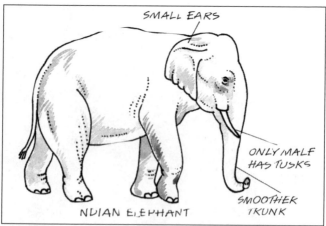

SMALL EARS

ONLY MALF HAS TUSKS

SMOOTHER TRUNK

NDIAN ELEPHANT

What kind of an elephant am I?
I'll give you a clue. *Big ears!*

A Little about Reading

When I want something I say, 'I wish …'

That's what they call *present tense*.

But suppose I made my wish last night? Then it's *past tense*. *'I wished...'*

It's easy to turn *present tense* into *past tense*.

Just add the two letters *ed*.

So *wish* becomes *wished*!

Except (there's always the odd word out) when it ends in *e*. Then you just add a *d*.

On pages 4 and 5 you'll find:

**mark-*ed*, temper-*ed*, foot-*ed*,
rule-*d*, divide-*d*, dare-*d*.**

See how it works!

But read the story first. Don't worry about words.

Fun before lessons!

Elephants – easy reading for new readers who have moved on a stage. Still with –

> *Large type*
> *Mostly short words*
> *Short sentences*
> *Lots of illustrations*
> *And fun!*

This is **Elephant 2.**
Elephant 1 is *The True Story of the Three Little Pigs and the Big Bad Wolf.*

Look out for more.

Pauline Devine was born in Loughrea, Co Galway. She now lives in Newcastle, Co Dublin, with her husband and daughter.

Her lifelong interest is in horses (she owns two). She is an exhibitor and prizewinner at the Kerrygold Dublin Horse Show and is active in local pony clubs.

The Hungry Horse is a revised edition of the book first published in 1988, which won her an Arts Council Bursary. Her other books are *Best Friends, Best Friends Again* and *Riders by the Grey Lake* (The Children's Press).

Terry Myler, one of Ireland's best-known illustrators, has also written *Drawing Made Easy* and *Drawing Made Very Easy.*